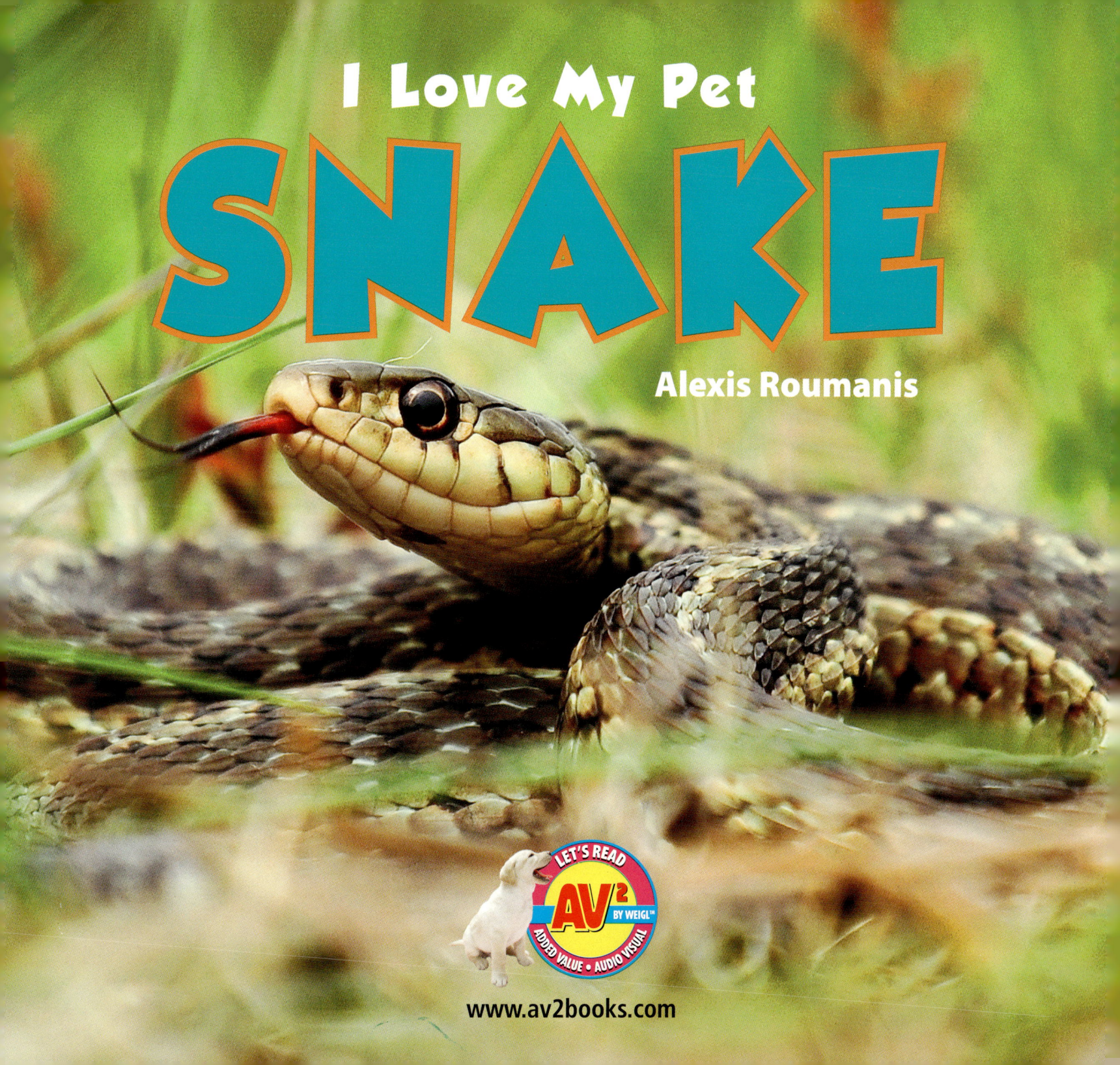

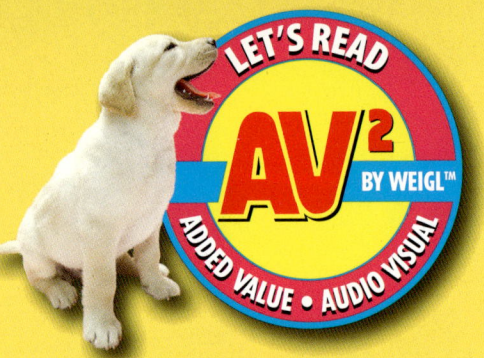

Go to www.av2books.com, and enter this book's unique code.

BOOK CODE

X215241

AV² by Weigl brings you media enhanced books that support active learning.

AV² provides enriched content that supplements and complements this book. Weigl's AV² books strive to create inspired learning and engage young minds in a total learning experience.

Your AV² Media Enhanced books come alive with...

 **Audio**
Listen to sections of the book read aloud.

 **Video**
Watch informative video clips.

 **Embedded Weblinks**
Gain additional information for research.

 **Try This!**
Complete activities and hands-on experiments.

 **Key Words**
Study vocabulary, and complete a matching word activity.

 **Quizzes**
Test your knowledge.

 **Slide Show**
View images and captions, and prepare a presentation.

... and much, much more!

Published by AV² by Weigl
350 5th Avenue, 59th Floor New York, NY 10118
Websites: www.av2books.com   www.weigl.com

Copyright ©2015 AV² by Weigl
All rights reserved. No part of this publication may be reproduced, stored in a retrieval system, or transmitted in any form or by any means, electronic, mechanical, photocopying, recording, or otherwise, without the prior written permission of the publisher.

Library of Congress Control Number: 2014934859
ISBN 978-1-4896-1298-4 (hardcover)
ISBN 978-1-4896-1299-1 (softcover)
ISBN 978-1-4896-1300-4 (single-user eBook)
ISBN 978-1-4896-1301-1 (multi-user eBook)

Printed in the United States of America in North Mankato, Minnesota
1 2 3 4 5 6 7 8 9 0 18 17 16 15 14

042014
WEP150314

Senior Editor: Aaron Carr   Art Director: Terry Paulhus

Weigl acknowledges Getty Images as the primary image supplier for this title.

I Love My Pet
SNAKE

CONTENTS

- 2 AV² Book Code
- 4 Snakes
- 6 Life Cycle
- 10 Features
- 14 Care
- 20 Health
- 22 Snake Facts
- 24 Key Words
- 24 www.av2books.com

3

I love my pet snake.
I take good care of him.

5

My pet snake hatched from an egg.
He could move around right after hatching.

My pet snake was three weeks old when I brought him home.
He will keep growing for his whole life.

Snakes can grow almost as long as a motorhome.

My pet snake has a good sense of smell.
He can smell with his tongue.

My pet snake sheds his old skin. It can take a few days for his skin to come off.

A snake sheds its skin about three times each year.

13

My pet snake needs help to stay warm.
He needs lights in his cage to keep him warm.

My pet snake eats bugs and small animals.
He likes to eat crickets and mice.

Snakes swallow their food whole.

My pet snake needs to be cared for. He needs fresh water to lie in every day.

19

I make sure my pet snake is healthy. I love my pet snake.

SNAKE FACTS

These pages provide more detail about the interesting facts found in the book. They are intended to be used by adults as a learning support to help young readers round out their knowledge of each animal featured in the *I Love My Pet* series.

Pages 4–5  **I love my pet snake. I take good care of him.** There are about 2,600 kinds of snakes in the world. About 400 of these snakes are poisonous. Most people keep non-poisonous snakes as pets. To stay healthy and happy, snakes need a clean cage, food, water, and exercise. They also need plenty of light, heat, and space. Each species of snake is different, so owners need to learn their snake's needs.

Pages 6–7  **My pet snake hatched from an egg. He could move around right after hatching.** Snakes are reptiles. Most reptiles lay eggs to have babies. When snakes hatch from their eggs, they are called snakelets. Many snakes develop an egg tooth before they hatch. The egg tooth projects forwards, and is used to break the egg open, from the inside. Shortly after hatching, the egg tooth is shed.

Pages 8–9  **My pet snake was three weeks old when I brought him home. He will keep growing for his whole life.** Many snakes are ready to live with their new owners right after hatching. Most snake parents do not take care of their young. Snakes must fend for themselves. Snakelets grow quickly until they reach maturity. When snakes reach maturity, they continue to grow at a slower rate.

Pages 10–11  **My pet snake has a good sense of smell. He can smell with his tongue.** Most snakes have poor eyesight. They make up for this with a keen sense of smell. When a snake sticks out its tongue, air particles collect on the tongue's surface. When the tongue goes back inside the mouth, the fork at the tip of the tongue touches the roof of the mouth. At the roof of the mouth is a sensory organ that helps the snake identify smells.

Pages 12–13

My pet snake sheds his old skin. It can take a few days for his skin to come off. The outer layer of a snake's skin does not grow. As a snake grows bigger, it needs to shed its old skin. This is called molting. A snake's eyes will look cloudy during this process, as snakes also shed a layer of skin that protects their eyes. Providing a moist environment can help the snake molt, but owners should not try to help pull the old skin off the snake. This could harm the snake.

Pages 14–15

My pet snake needs help to stay warm. He needs lights in his cage to keep him warm. As cold blooded animals, snakes cannot make their own heat to stay warm. Instead, snakes must sit in sunlight to warm up or dip into water to cool off. A pet snake needs special heat lights in its cage.

Pages 16–17

My pet snake eats bugs and small animals. He likes to eat crickets and mice. Snakes are carnivores, or meat eaters. Most snakes eat insects, birds, eggs, rodents, frogs, fish, lizards, and small mammals. Many pet owners feed their snakes frozen mice. Depending on the species, snakes can go up to several weeks between feedings.

Pages 18–19

My pet snake needs to be cared for. He needs fresh water to lie in every day. Without water, it only takes a few days for a snake to become dehydrated. Snakes can absorb water through their skin. A small water dish in a snake's cage will allow the snake to hydrate when needed. The water depth should only be twice as high as the height of the snake, so that the snake does not drown.

Pages 20–21

I make sure my pet snake is healthy. I love my pet snake. Keeping a snake healthy and happy is a big job. The cage needs to be cleaned at least once a week. Pet owners should also ensure the water dish is kept clean. Uneaten food should be removed from the cage a few hours after feeding. Taking time every day to play with the snake and give it exercise is also important to its health.

23

KEY WORDS

Research has shown that as much as 65 percent of all written material published in English is made up of 300 words. These 300 words cannot be taught using pictures or learned by sounding them out. They must be recognized by sight. This book contains 59 common sight words to help young readers improve their reading fluency and comprehension. This book also teaches young readers several important content words, such as proper nouns. These words are paired with pictures to aid in learning and improve understanding.

Page	Sight Words First Appearance
4	good, him, I, my, of, take
6	after, an, around, could, from, he, move, right
9	a, almost, as, can, for, grow, his, home, keep, life, long, old, three, was, when, will
11	has, with
12	about, come, days, each, few, it, its, off, times, to, year
15	help, in, lights, needs
16	and, animals, eats, food, likes, small, their
18	be, every, water
21	is, make

Page	Content Words First Appearance
4	snake
6	egg
9	motorhome, weeks
11	sense, smell, tongue
12	skin
15	cage
16	bugs, crickets, mice

Check out www.av2books.com for activities, videos, audio clips, and more!

1) Go to www.av2books.com.
2) Enter book code.   X 2 1 5 2 4 1
3) Fuel your imagination online!

www.av2books.com